# WHAT IF . . . ?

# THEN WE . . .

Short, Very Short, Shorter-than-Ever Possibilities

**REBECCA KAI DOTLICH**  Illustrated by **FRED KOEHLER**

BOYDS MILLS PRESS
AN IMPRINT OF HIGHLIGHTS
*Honesdale, Pennsylvania*

For every **WHAT IF,** the imagination creates a possibility,

and in that possibility lives a story.

# WHAT IF...

we got lost far, far, far away,
and couldn't find our way home?

# THEN WE

would become
the bravest explorers
in the world.

# WHAT IF ...

## the clocks stopped ticktocking?

# THEN WE

would have no bedtime.

# WHAT IF . . .

every crayon in the world melted?

# THEN WE

would grab our pencils
and fall in love with gray.

# WHAT IF . . .

we began to cry and cry
and could not stop?

# THEN WE

would make our own ocean
to sail and
fish for dreams.

# THEN WE

would invent a
whole new language.

# WHAT IF . . .

we get mad and never, ever, ever talk again?

**THEN WE**

would miss all the things
that we would
never, ever, ever
share again.

# WHAT IF...
something *really* big and
*really* scary happened?

# THEN WE

would whistle and
hold hands until . . .

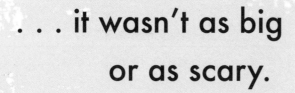

. . . it wasn't as big
or as scary.

# WHAT IF . . .

we shared something amazing
and magnificent and wonderful?

# THEN WE

would keep it our secret,
and treasure it every day.

WHAT IF ...

we wanted to imagine
a thousand more possibilities?

THEN WE WOULD!

To young writers, creators, and makers
who imagine possibilities
and fish for dreams.

*And to Mom, who loves clocks.*
*I will love you till the end of time.*
*—RKD*

For Mom
—FK

Boyds Mills Press
An Imprint of Highlights
815 Church Street
Honesdale, Pennsylvania 18431
Printed in China

ISBN: 978-1-62979-909-4
Library of Congress Control Number: 2018906274

First edition
10 9 8 7 6 5 4 3 2 1

Design by Barbara Grzeslo
The text of this book is set in Rather Loud bold and Futura medium.
The titles are set in Rather Loud bold.
The illustrations are created in mixed media.